THE MYSTERY

Maxwell Eaton III

Alfred A. Knopf · New York

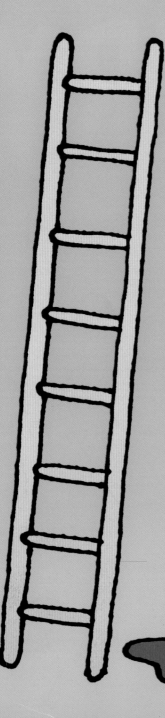

To Kristin

THIS IS A BORZOI BOOK PUBLISHED BY ALFRED A. KNOPF

Copyright © 2008 by Maxwell Eaton III

Knopf, Borzoi Books, and the colophon are registered trademarks of Random House, Inc.

Visit us on the Web! www.randomhouse.com/kids

Educators and librarians, for a variety of teaching tools, visit us at www.randomhouse.com/teachers

Library of Congress Cataloging-in-Publication Data
Eaton, Maxwell.
The mystery / by Maxwell Eaton III. — 1st ed.
p.   cm. — (The adventures of Max and Pinky)
Summary: Max and his best friend Pinky the pig decide to paint the barn, but when it turns up repainted
the next morning, they must find out what happened.
ISBN 978-0-375-83807-1 (trade) — ISBN 978-0-375-93807-8 (lib. bdg.)
[1. Best friends—Fiction. 2. Friendship—Fiction. 3. Domestic animals—Fiction. 4. Pigs—Fiction.
5. Mystery and detective stories.] I. Title.
PZ7.E3892My 2008
[E]—dc22
2007044313

The illustrations in this book were created using black pen-and-ink with digital coloring.

MANUFACTURED IN CHINA

October 2008

10 9 8 7 6 5 4 3 2 1

First Edition

Max and Pinky are going to paint the barn.

and finish just before it gets dark.

Morning comes.
What will Max and Pinky do today?

It takes all day to repaint the barn.

They stay up all night to guard it.

But in the morning, there's a new surprise.

Max and Pinky repaint **AGAIN** and set out to solve the mystery.

They look for clues.

They ask tough questions.

But the mysterious painter can't be found.

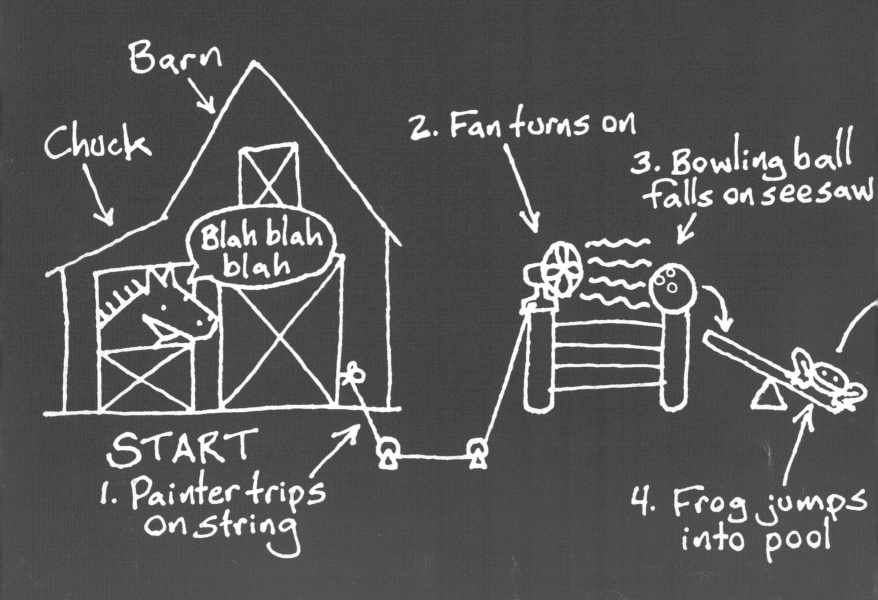

BARN ALARM
BY Max and Pinky
by Pinky + max
7. Duck quacks
Quack
M
P
POOL
House
5. Splashes chicken
6. Chicken pulls string

That night, everyone is fast asleep.

**Suddenly, the alarm goes off!
But where is Pinky?**

Max runs outside to find . . .

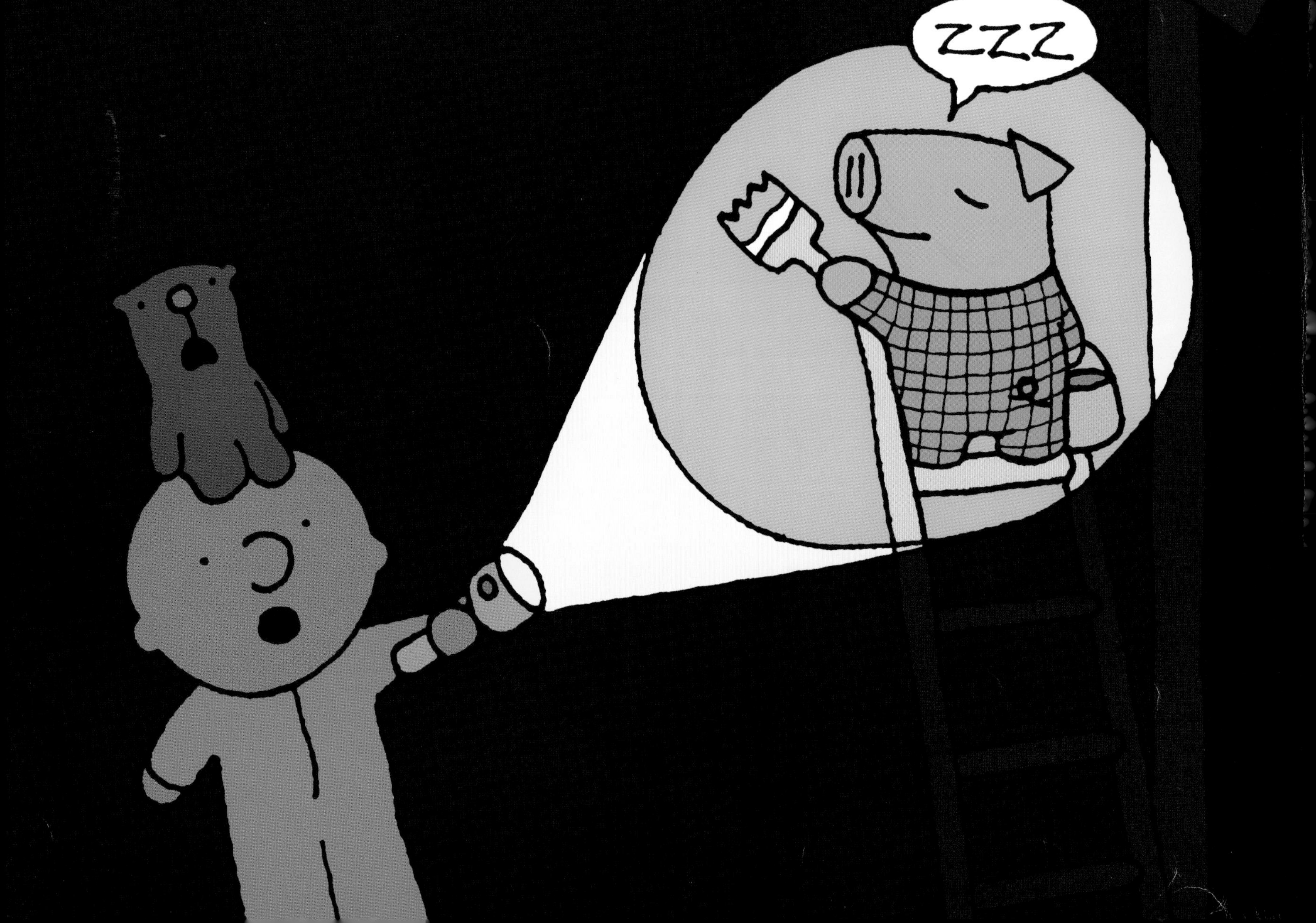

Pinky has been painting the barn in his sleep.

Max gently walks Pinky back to bed.

In the morning, they head
out to the barn and . . .

one of them is surprised.

Max makes a suggestion.

But Pinky will never give up!

The adventures continue.